CW01175665

All About Animals

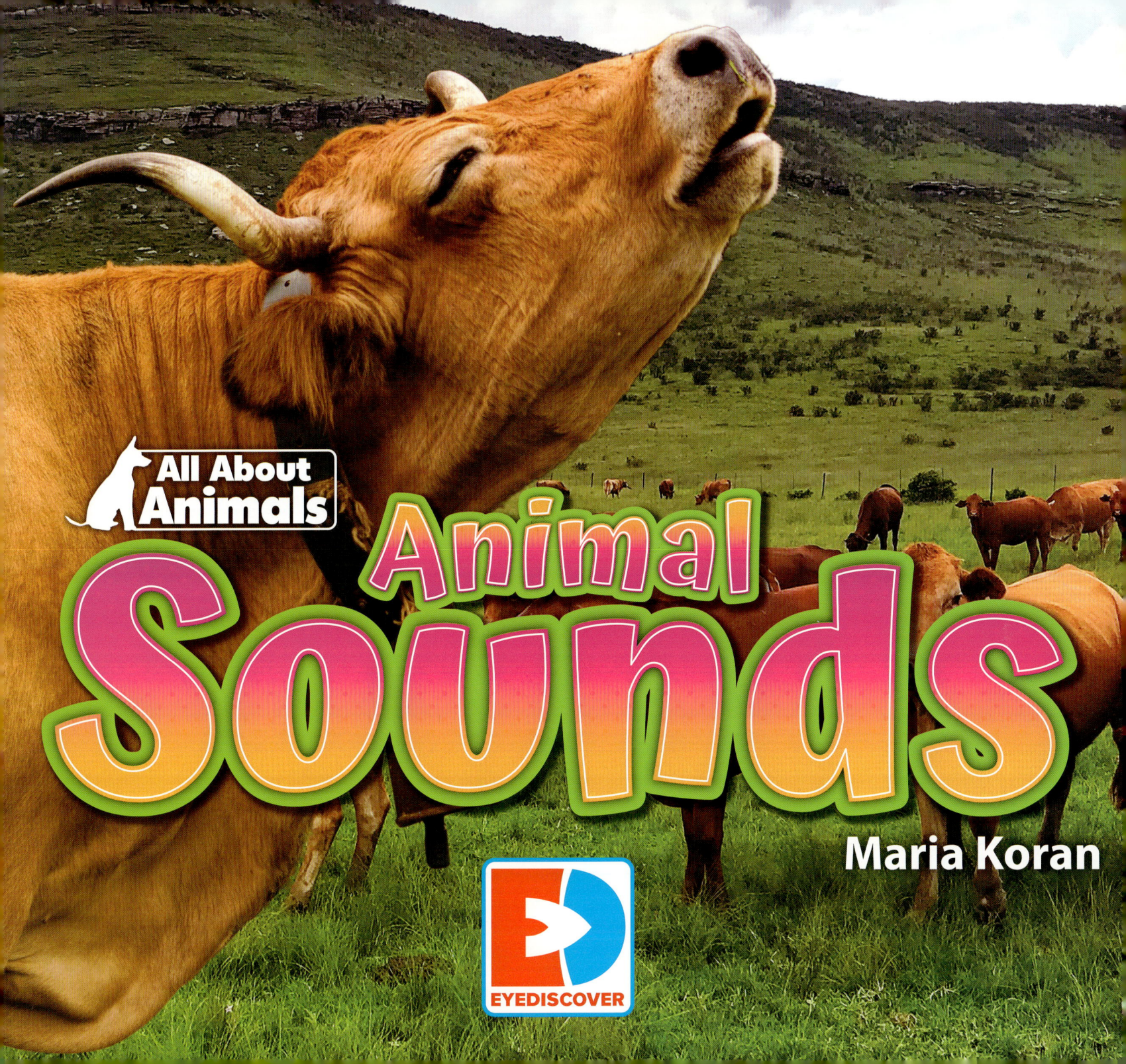

Animal Sounds

Maria Koran

EYEDISCOVER

EYEDISCOVER

Go to **www.eyediscover.com** and enter this book's unique code.

BOOK CODE

AVU48678

EYEDISCOVER brings you optic readalongs that support active learning.

Published by AV² by Weigl
350 5th Avenue, 59th Floor New York, NY 10118
Website: www.eyediscover.com

Copyright ©2020 AV² by Weigl
All rights reserved. No part of this publication may be reproduced, stored in a retrieval system, or transmitted in any form or by any means, electronic, mechanical, photocopying, recording, or otherwise, without the prior written permission of the publisher.

Library of Congress Control Number: 2019946278

ISBN 978-1-7911-0740-6 (hardcover)

Printed in Guangzhou, China
1 2 3 4 5 6 7 8 9 0 23 22 21 20 19

072019
121818

Project Coordinator: John Willis
Designers: Mandy Christiansen and Ana María Vidal

Weigl acknowledges Alamy, Getty Images, iStock, and Minden Pictures as the primary image suppliers for this title.

EYEDISCOVER provides enriched content, optimized for tablet use, that supplements and complements this book. EYEDISCOVER books strive to create inspired learning and engage young minds in a total learning experience.

Watch
Video content brings each page to life.

Browse
Thumbnails make navigation simple.

Read
Follow along with text on the screen.

Listen
Hear each page read aloud.

Your EYEDISCOVER Optic Readalongs come alive with...

Audio
Listen to the entire book read aloud.

Video
High resolution videos turn each spread into an optic readalong.

OPTIMIZED FOR
☑ TABLETS
☑ WHITEBOARDS
☑ COMPUTERS
☑ AND MUCH MORE!

2

Animal Sounds

In this book, you will learn about

- what they are called

- what they are for

and much more!

Many animals make sounds. Lions roar to show their strength.

5

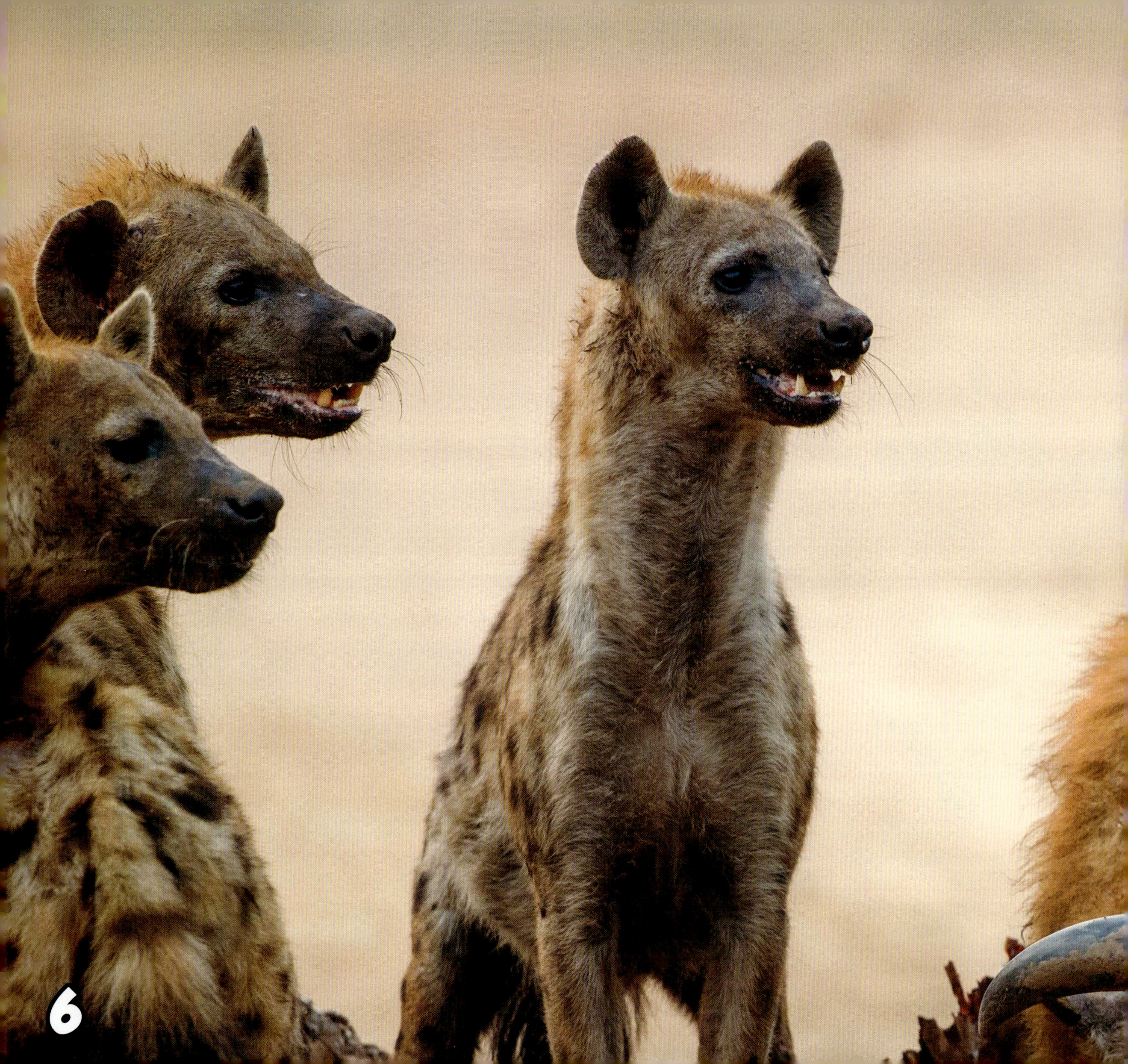

Hyenas make many sounds. Some of them sound like laughter.

Baboons grunt and bark. Sometimes, they scream.

9

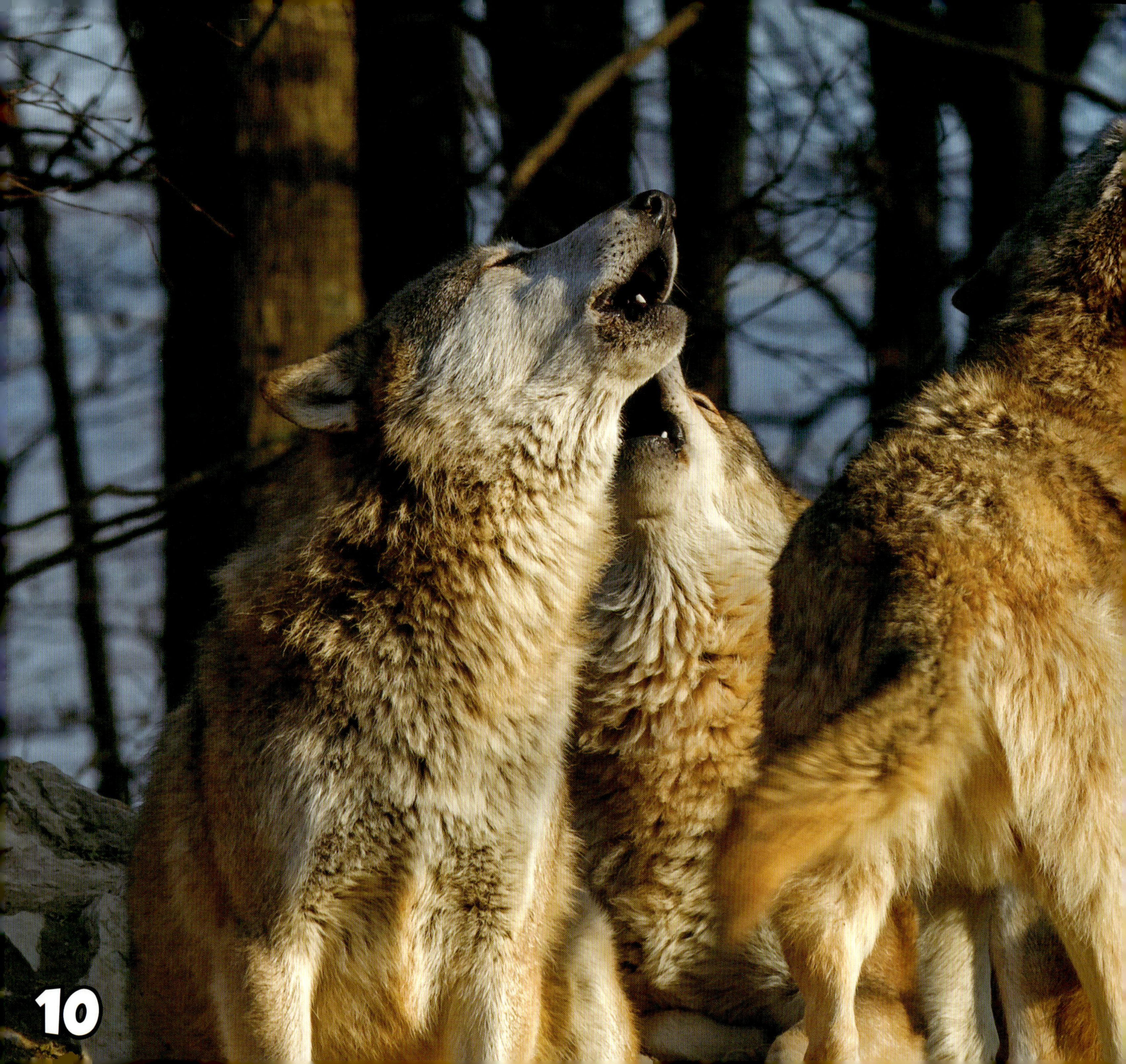

Wolves howl to help other wolves find them.

Rattlesnakes shake their tails to make noise. This lets other animals know to stay away.

12

13

14

Some whales talk by singing. Different groups have different songs.

Elephants trumpet loudly. This helps them warn each other of danger.

17

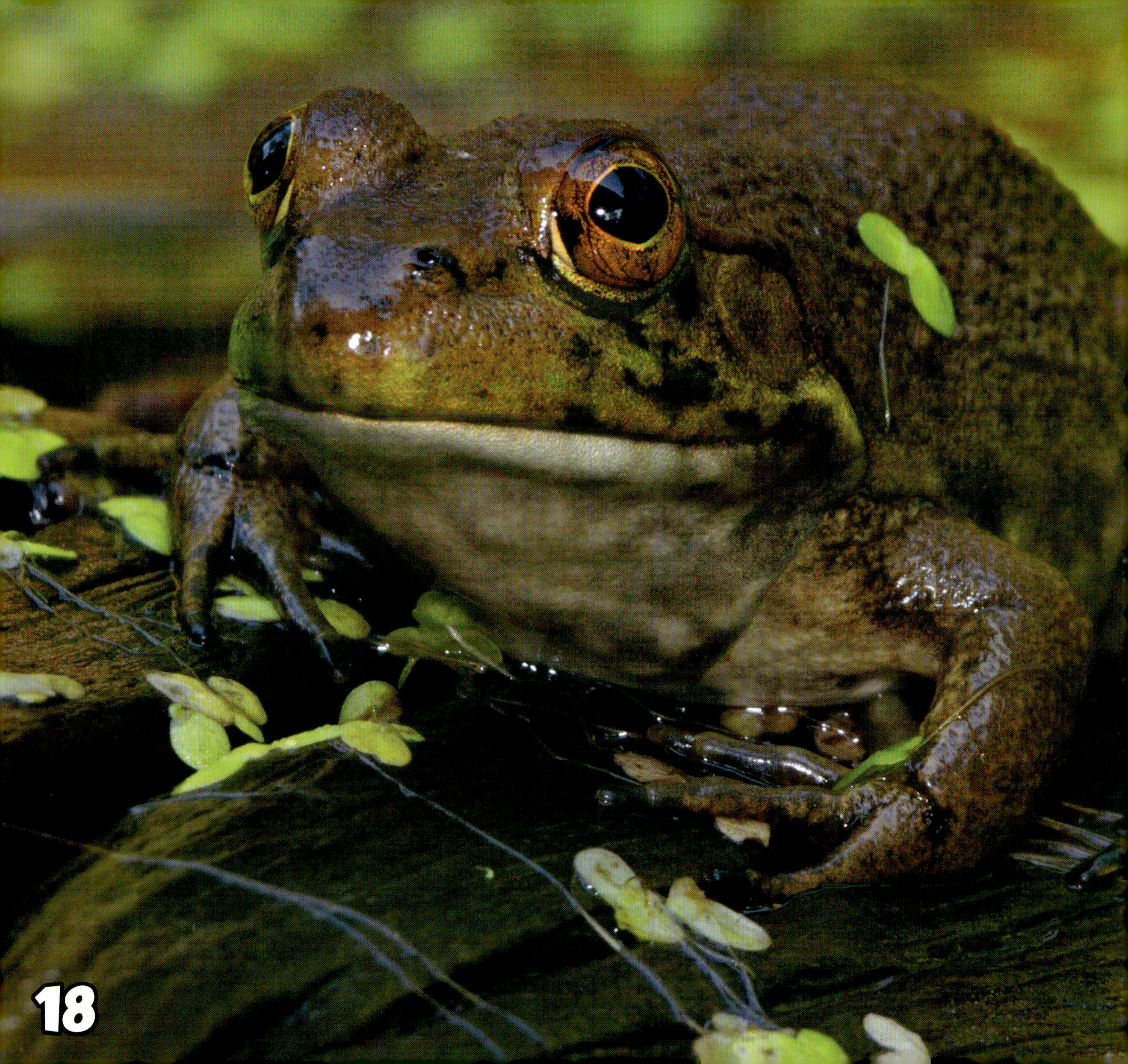

Bullfrogs are named for their loud calls. They sound like cows.

Birds can be very noisy. Parrots whistle, chatter, and sing when they are happy.

21

ANIMAL SOUNDS BY THE NUMBERS

A **lion's roar** can be heard from **5 miles** away.
(8 kilometers)

Spotted hyenas are also known as **laughing hyenas**. They can weigh up to **190 pounds**.
(86 kilograms)

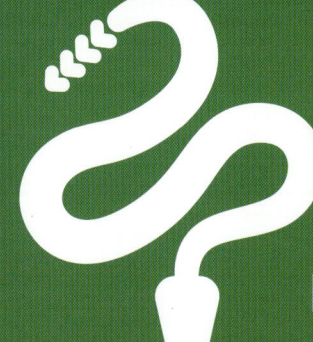

There are at least **30 different** kinds of **rattlesnakes**.

A **wolf** pack's **territory** can cover **1,200 square miles.** (3,100 square km)

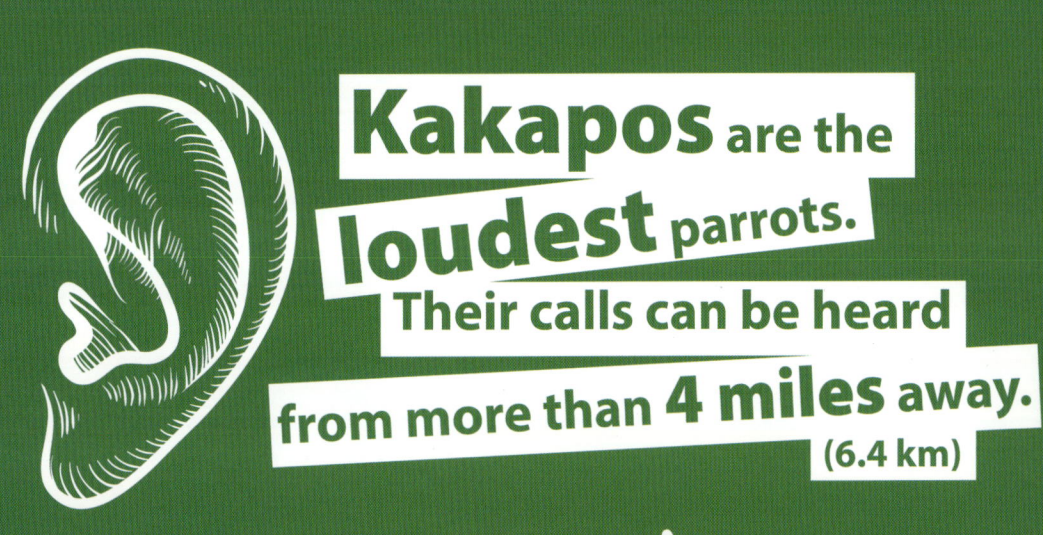

Kakapos are the **loudest** parrots. Their calls can be heard from more than **4 miles** away. (6.4 km)

A **blue whale's call** reaches **188 decibels.** This is **louder** than a **jet engine.**

KEY WORDS

Research has shown that as much as 65 percent of all written material published in English is made up of 300 words. These 300 words cannot be taught using pictures or learned by sounding them out. They must be recognized by sight. This book contains 35 common sight words to help young readers improve their reading fluency and comprehension. This book also teaches young readers several important content words, such as proper nouns. These words are paired with pictures to aid in learning and improve understanding.

Page	Sight Words First Appearance
4	animals, make, many, show, sounds, their, to
7	like, of, some, them
8	and, sometimes, they
11	find, help, other
12	away, know, lets, this
15	by, different, groups, have, songs, talk
16	each
19	are, calls, for
20	be, can, very, when

Page	Content Words First Appearance
4	lions, roar, strength
7	hyenas, laughter
8	baboons, bark, grunt, scream
11	howl, wolves
12	noise, rattlesnakes, tails
15	singing, whales
16	danger, elephants, trumpet
19	bullfrogs, cows
20	birds, chatter, parrots, whistle

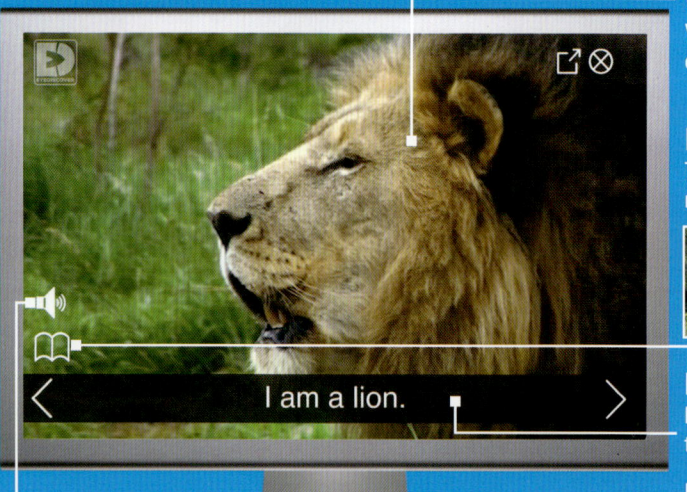

Watch
Video content brings each page to life.

Browse
Thumbnails make navigation simple.

Read
Follow along with text on the screen.

Listen
Hear each page read aloud.

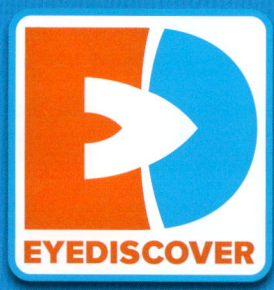

EYEDISCOVER

Go to www.eyediscover.com and enter this book's unique code.

BOOK CODE

AVU48678

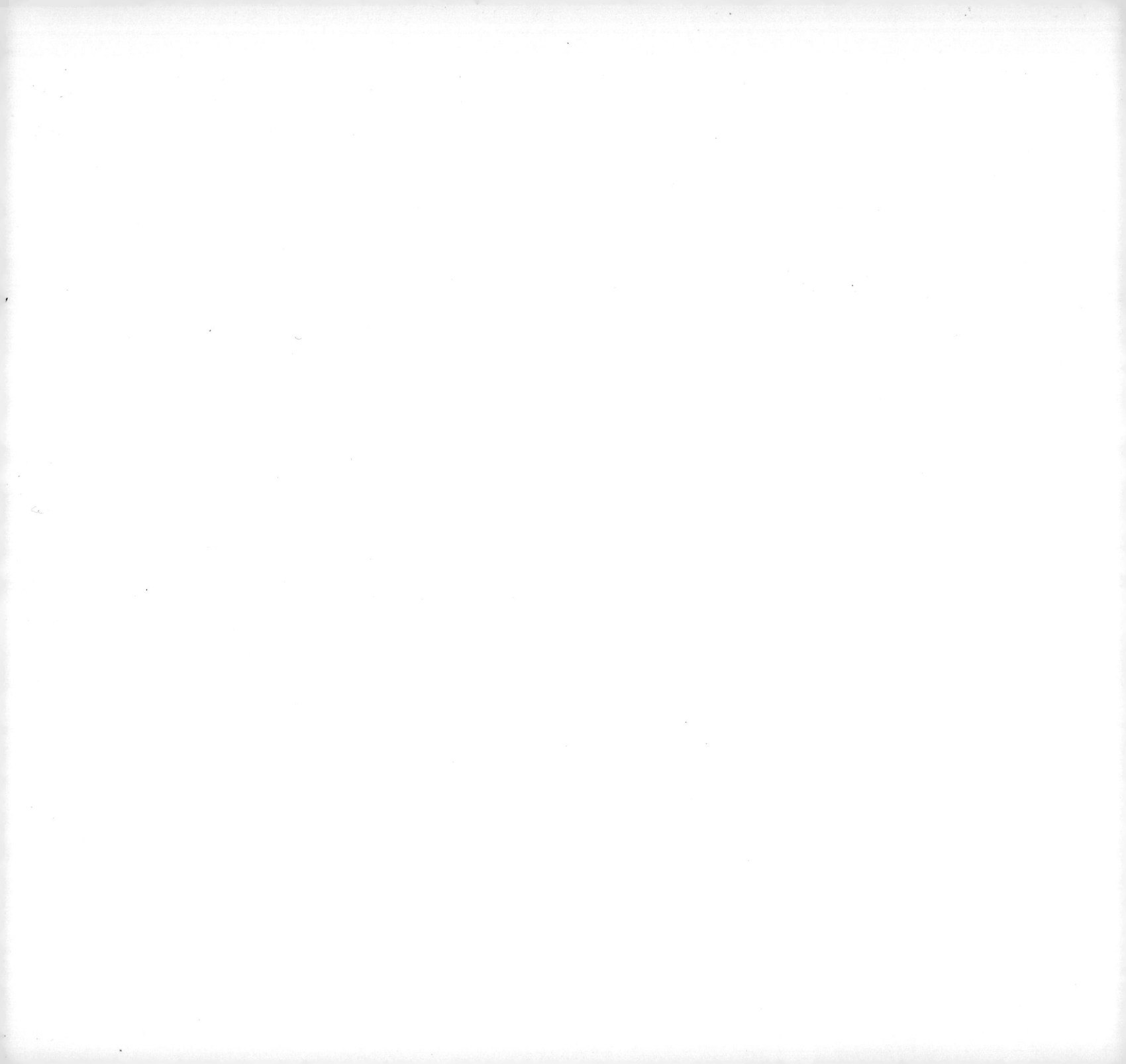